La Cucaracha Martina doesn't like life in the big city. The loud city sounds hurt her tiny ears and keep her awake at night. Determined to find the source of the one *beautiful* noise she has heard only a few times, Martina takes to the town! On street upon street, this very little cockroach creates ever so big a stir. One after another, animals come to catch a glimpse of this ravishing roach. Soon, marriage proposals fly and love is in the air.

Dog barks . . .

WOOF! WOOF!

And Pig huffs . . .

OINK! OINK!

But none of their noises will do.

Who will win the heart of this most extraordinary cucarachita?

Turtle Books

La Cucaracha Martina

First published in 1997 by Turtle Books
First softcover edition published in 1999
by Turtle Books

Book & cover design by Daniel Moreton

The illustrations in this book were
created on an Apple™ Macintosh
using Adobe™ Illustrator.

First Softcover Edition
Printed on 80# Mountie white, acid-free paper
Printed and bound in the United States of America
10 9 8 7 6 5 4 3 2 1

Turtle Books, 866 United Nations Plaza, Suite 525, New York, NY 10017

Library of Congress
Cataloging-in-Publication Data
Moreton, Daniel.
La Cucaracha Martina :
a Caribbean folktale / retold and illustrated
by Daniel Moreton. p. cm.
Summary: While searching for the source of one
beautiful sound, a ravishing cockroach rejects marriage
proposals from a menagerie of city animals which woo her
with their noises.
ISBN 1-890515-03-5 (hardcover : alk. paper)
ISBN 1-890515-17-5 (softcover : alk.paper)
[1. Folklore–Caribbean Area. 2. Cockroaches–Folklore.
3. Animal sounds–Folklore. 4. Noise–Folklore.]
I. Title. PZ8. 1.M815Cu 1997
398.2'09729'04525728–dc21
97-13631 CIP AC

Distributed by
Publishers Group West

ISBN 1-890515-17-5

La Cucaracha Martina

A Caribbean Folktale

retold and illustrated by
Daniel Moreton

Turtle Books New York

HONK!
HONK!
HONK!
AUTOBÚS
TELÉFONO
PARE
RING!
RING!

AEROPUERTO

CAFÉ
TAMALES
FRUTA
AGUACATES
CHORIZO
GUANÁBANA
SHAKES

La Cucaracha Martina didn't care much for life in the big city. She didn't like the animals who hung out on the street corner and the thought of getting stepped on frightened her terribly.

But it was the noise that Martina liked the least. The loud city sounds hurt her tiny ears and kept her awake at night.

On special nights, however, when all else was still, Martina would hear a *beautiful* noise, a soft gentle sound that came whispering through the night. It was the most fabulous noise she had ever heard and it made her feel all funny inside.

Early one Monday morning, La Cucaracha Martina decided to fix herself up and go out in search of the beautiful noise. She took some money over to the market and purchased—

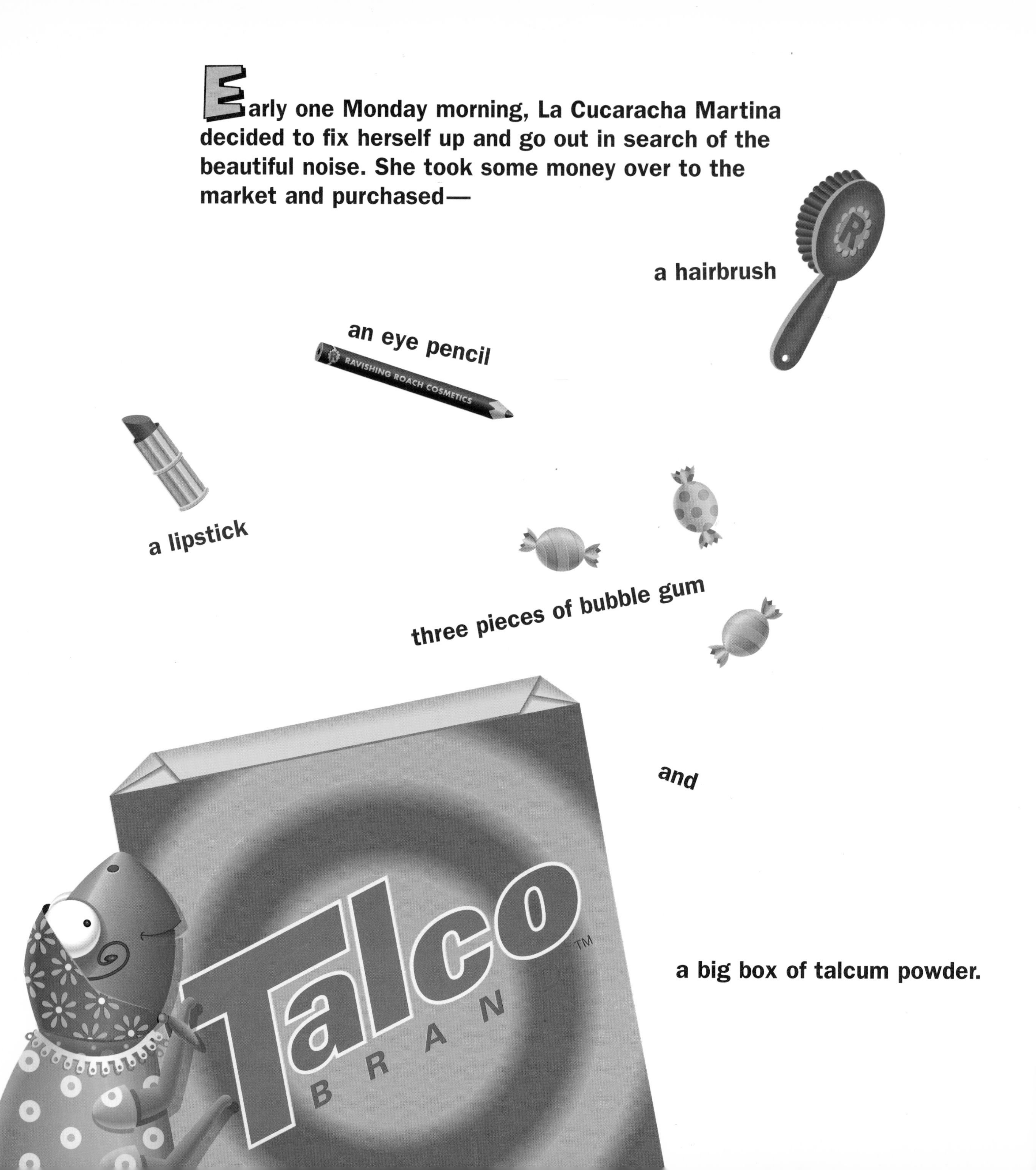

a hairbrush

an eye pencil

a lipstick

three pieces of bubble gum

and

a big box of talcum powder.

Martina worked quickly. She brushed her hair and fixed her face. She shined her shoes and buttoned up her best dress.

PUFF! PUFF! PUFF!

POOF! POOF!

Never before had there been a more beautiful cucaracha.

By the time the noon whistle blew, Martina was out in search of the beautiful noise. She hadn't gone but one block when she was stopped by Dog.

"Good afternoon, Cucaracha Martina!" said Dog. "You look especially lovely today."

"Thank you," said La Cucaracha, clutching her purse.

"Would you marry me?" asked Dog smiling.

"Oh, I couldn't possibly," answered Martina. "I'm looking for a beautiful noise."

"A beautiful noise?" asked Dog.

And Dog went . . .

108 C

WOOF!
WOOF!

"That's a terrible noise!" snapped Martina,

and she scurried off down the street.

La Cucaracha Martina was well on her way, when Pig suddenly blocked her path.

"Excuse me!" said La Cucaracha.

"No, excuse me!" squealed Pig. "For you are the most marvelous cucaracha I have ever seen. Would you marry me?"

"I can't marry you," said Martina. "You're a pig! And besides, I'm looking for a beautiful noise."

"A beautiful noise?" huffed Pig.

And Pig went . . .

"What a horrible noise," said La Cucaracha Martina, and she darted off down the block.

Soon after, Rooster came racing by La Cucaracha Martina.

"Pardon me, sightly senorita, you are a most gorgeous cucarachita," said Rooster. "Would you marry me?"

"I don't think I can, you see, I'm looking for a beautiful noise."

"A beautiful noise?" crowed Rooster.

And Rooster went . . .

cock-a-doodleee doodleee doodleee doodleee doo!

"My! That's quite a noise," said Martina, and she went off in search of the beautiful noise.

Days passed and La Cucaracha Martina became the talk of the town. All eyes were on her as she shuffled down the street. Animals came from all over just to get a look at the ravishing roach in search of the beautiful noise.

25
SSSSSSSSSSSSS
QUACK!
QUACK!
QUACK!
SAL
Azúcar
CCROAK!
CCCCCC
MEOW

There was Bird . . .
CHIRP!
CHIRP!
CHIRP!
CHIRP!

and Mouse . . .

SQUEAK!
SQUEAK!
SQUEAK!
SQUEAK!

and Bull all the way from Brazil!

mooooo

clank! clank!

Weeks passed and La Cucaracha Martina thought only of the beautiful noise. No other sound would satisfy her . . .

not Fish,

GURGLE, GURGLE, glub, glub!

not Flea,

PEEP!

PEEP!

BUZZZZZZ
not even Bee.

ZZZZZZZZZ
MIEL

Months passed and La Cucaracha Martina longed only to hear again the beautiful noise. She wanted to continue the search, but her six tiny feet could walk no further.

It was on this very night,
while getting ready for bed,
that La Cucaracha Martina
heard a familiar noise,
a soft, gentle noise,
a beautiful noise.

It was in fact *the* beautiful
noise! It grew stronger
and even more beautiful
until it filled the whole
room. Martina, beside
herself with joy,
stumbled over
to the window.

There, on the streetlamp below, was a tiny cricket making the most beautiful noise anyone had ever heard.

“Good evening,” creaked Cricket.

“Good evening,” sighed La Cucaracha Martina.

“You are the most beautiful cucaracha I have ever seen,” serenaded Cricket.

“And *you* make the most beautiful noise I’ve ever heard,” cried La Cucaracha. “Will you marry me?”

sang Cricket.

“Yes I will.”

And so they were wed. . . .

Family and friends came creeping and crawling from all over just to witness this sensational sight. From Uncle Ernie to Aunt Hortensia, everyone agreed— the wedding was a spectacular success!

CERTIFICADO
ARROZ

Not long after, La Cucaracha and Cricket moved away. They went off to the country, where a cockroach and a cricket could enjoy the sounds of silence. At night they would play bingo, make cocoa, and stare at the stars. And sometimes, on special nights, when all else was still, they would fill the night with beautiful noise.

Daniel Moreton graduated from the Rhode Island School of Design, in 1991, with a degree in illustration. He also studied at the Instituto de Allende in Guanajuato, Mexico, where the art and culture of Mexico became a fresh inspiration for his work.

Daniel's own Cuban heritage is a continuing source of inspiration. Childhood memories of stories told him by his grandmother became the source for *La Cucaracha Martina*. And his first book, *Martí and the Mango*—an original tale about Martí the mouse in search of a mysterious mango—also reflects his Cuban background.

Daniel, an illustrator and designer, lives in New York City with his dog, Gomez. Like Martina, Gomez doesn't care much for life in the big city. He, too, often dreams of a more quiet life in the country.

La Cucaracha Martina is also available in Spanish editions,
La Cucaracha Martina: un cuento folklórico del Caribe
Hardcover ISBN 1-890515-04-3 Softcover ISBN 1-890515-18-3

Book printed in the United States of America

Distributed by Publishers Group West

Visit our home page on the World Wide Web:
www.turtlebooks.com

Turtle Books
866 United Nations Plaza, Suite 525
New York, New York 10017